BAD ENGLISH

DOGG PACK SERIES

EVIE MITCHELL

THUNDER THIGHS PUBLISHING

Editor: Nicole Wilson, Evermore Editing
http://www.evermoreediting.wixsite.com/info

ACKNOWLEDGEMENT OF COUNTRY

I acknowledge the Traditional Custodians of the lands on which I write, the Ngunnawal people, and pay my respect to elders both past and present.

I acknowledge the continued and deep spiritual relationship of the Australian Aboriginal and Torres Strait Islander peoples' to this land, and their unique cultural and spiritual relationships to the land, waters and seas and their rich contribution to society.

Always was, always will be.

To my Greedy Reader group,

You are the best place on the internet.
Books, memes and laughs.
Thank you for supporting me to write the kind
of books you love—even if you all demand more!

And as always, to my husband.
A man who reads is a many splendid thing.
But a man who enables you to read and write?
That sir is a keeper.

BAD ENGLISH

The first chapter of my happily ever after just walked into my class... only he's competing for my job. Talk about a plot twist.

Enid

I'm not the kind of woman people remember. Or talk about. Or see. I mean, I've been mistaken for a chair—more than once.

I was okay being a wallflower, a bluestocking, a spinster-in-waiting. I dedicated myself to my work, and I was satisfied with my life. Happy even.

Or at least I was, until Henry.

Now I want to be seen. I want the love story. I want the hero who only has eyes for me.

Except he's been invited to apply for the job I was promised. As perfect as this romance-reading-tea-sipping-Brit may be, there's no way in hell I'm letting him win.

I thought this would be our love story. I think it's about to turn into a true crime.

CHAPTER 1

Enid

"I am powerful. I am strong. I am knowledgeable. I am enough."

I stared at the woman in the mirror, trying to find an ounce of the confidence and self-possession my words contained.

Mousy brown hair that had a tendency to frizz, thick glasses framing plain brown eyes, pale skin painted with a smattering of freckles across the bridge of a too-big nose. The rest of my body matched my nose— lips far too big for my face, curves too generous sat on a body shaped less like an hourglass and more like a slightly dimply rectangle.

I opened my mouth, reciting the mantra again.

"I am powerful. I am strong. I am knowledgeable. I am enough."

I squinted at myself, hoping to see a little bubble of... change, perhaps? Maybe even a little glow as my body presented externally with a new level of confidence.

Instead, an eyelash fluttered to land on my cheek.

I sighed, lifting my glasses to brush the stray away.

Maybe tomorrow.

With determination, I straightened my shoulders, shoving away from the sink.

"Today I am the master of my own destiny."

I needed to believe that. I needed the confidence and the assurance that I could control the outcomes of the next six weeks.

"Enid? Are you okay?" My roommate's muffled question floated through the closed door, followed by a gentle knock. "Should I be worried? You've been in there an awfully long time."

"I'm fine, Keiko. Just... thinking."

I could feel her unasked question radiating through the door.

What are you thinking so hard about?

My answer would be something fluffy, like my next lecture, or what books I'd assign my students to read during the holiday break. But in reality, my thoughts were a cycle of torment, and all because of one sweet-talking-romance-reading-deliciously-gorgeous-tea-sipping-literary-master Brit.

Henry Tenil. The superstar from across the pond.

"Alright," Keiko said finally, her tone implying that all was not right. "I'm leaving for work. Call if you need anything, okay?"

"Will do!" I tried to inject positivity into my voice knowing I probably sounded as ridiculous as I felt. "Have a nice day."

"You too."

I listened as she bumped around the house for a moment, then closed our front door, silence descending in her wake.

"Okay, Enid. It's time to woman up. Let's put on the grandmother underwear and come to terms with what is about to happen. You're about to meet the man who you've fantasized about for years. You're about to meet a man who makes your insides watery. You're about to meet the one person in the world who convinced you to sign up for social media."

I swallowed, seeing the flush on my cheeks.

"You can't fangirl. You can't freak out. You need to be professional—not starry-eyed. You can do this, Enid. You're a badass bitch." I paused, not liking that term. "Scratch that. You're a badass boss woman who knows exactly what she wants and is willing to work to get it. And Henry being here is just another step to getting what you want. And what do we want?" I leaned into the mirror, giving myself a squinty-eyed glare. "Tenure. We've worked too hard for too long to allow this to all fall to pieces because of a little crush."

Or not so little, if I'm honest.

"Let's get over our infatuation the only way one truly can—by meeting their hero and being solidly underwhelmed by the experience."

I considered myself in the mirror for a moment.

Do I believe any of that?

"Yes, I do.'" With a brisk nod, I left the bathroom, shoulders back, head high—only to promptly slip on a stray sock left by Keiko's cat.

My legs slipped out from under me, my body flying through the air, and on the way down to the polished wood floor, I had only one thing I knew for sure.

This isn't a good sign.

CHAPTER 2

Henry

I studied the long drive of the small but prestigious university, feeling a little like a boy on his first day at school.

College, remember? They call them colleges over here.

The old willow trees lining the drive drooped, the sun playing hide-and-seek with their leaves, dotting the road in a veritable speckle of shade and light.

Terrible wording. Can't use that in a book.

"You a student here?" the Uber driver asked as we coasted down the lane.

"A research fellow, actually."

"Ah," the driver said, scratching his forehead. "Important then?"

I chuckled, shaking my head. "Afraid not. I'm just here to teach a few classes and finish some research."

The sweet sizzle of anticipation began to hum in my blood, my fingers itching to begin.

So close.

I'd been researching the early 1700s writer Cedric Cagle for the past ten years. I'd discovered him while finishing my thesis on gendered writing and the proliferation of male pen names by magnificent female authors from the early 1700s to late 1900s.

I'd been chasing leads and rabbit holes for years in an effort to prove that Cedric Cagle was actually Mary Allen, a young Scottish-Astipian immigrant. Cedric was also reportedly a Scottish-Astipian, whose published works bore an astounding similarity to Mary's.

I'd uncovered her during my thesis research while in Scotland and fallen in love. I'd tracked her to the Kingdom of Astipia but all traces of the magnificent woman had been wiped clean upon her arrival in Astipia. There wasn't even a death certificate or marriage license to trace.

Then I'd discovered Cedric. The works were brilliant, witty, female-centric, and somehow reportedly written by a man. I'd done what I could through my ongoing research, but the majority of Cedric's works had yet to be digitalized, which had meant I'd hit a dead end.

Until now.

The car passed an enormous building, the old weathered stone marked with moss and climbing ivy. A sign stood in front of the building, proudly proclaiming it the *Whitfield Library.*

There it is.

The giant building contained a wealth of resources—but, most importantly, housed a rare book collection that rivalled that anywhere in the world, left to the college by its titled benefactor. These rare books were lovingly cared for and curated by a team of exceptional historians. And soon, I would get to be among them, delving into the entire collection of Cedric Cagle.

Goosebumps rose on my skin as I rubbed my hands together, eager to begin.

Calm, Henry. The books will wait until tomorrow.

The campus was far smaller than some I'd toured over the years, but its situation was magnificent. Set outside the town of Capricorn Cove and just an hour's drive from the closest major city, the campus offered a surprising variety of courses, including marine biology, arts, literature, business, and agriculture. It felt like a mishmash of doctrines that had found a welcome home in the foothills of the coastal landscape.

"This is it," the driver said, interrupting my introspection. "Nice view."

Built just outside the college grounds were a row of small but tidy townhouses intended for the academic staff, beyond which nestled the softly undulating ocean.

"Well," I said, staring out at the view. "This is rather pleasant."

"You need a hand with your bags?" the driver asked.

"Thank you, but no. I'll get it."

And I don't want you touching my books.

I unloaded on the sidewalk, lifting a hand in thanks as the driver pulled away. With hands-on-hips, I surveyed the small townhouse, breathing in the salty air, and relishing the warm breeze on my cheeks.

I grinned, reading the sign on the door. "To quote Jane Austen, 'I dare say this is very agreeable.'"

And with a flourish, I pushed open the door to *Pemberley* and began to settle into my temporary home.

CHAPTER 3

Henry

"And this is our library." The Dean of Arts and Sciences, Linda Witcher, swept a hand out, encompassing the vast space. "No doubt you'll spend a number of hours lost between the stacks."

I chuckled, unable to deny her comment. My soul felt lighter as I stepped into the space, breathing in the familiar musty-sweet smell of well-worn books.

I'd spent last night getting settled in my new home. Books were shelved, the bed was dressed, and a grocery list a mile long was formed. Tea, it seemed, was not a staple in the land of thick, black coffee.

My morning had been taken up by a

conversation with the Dean, followed by a tour of the campus. We'd be meeting the faculty staff for a morning tea shortly, but first I wanted nothing more than to view the rare books. Being so close to works of art always got my blood pumping.

"If you'll follow me?" She led me through the building, explaining the layout and history of the library.

"And back here is our rare book collection. It's—"

Her phone rang interrupting her.

"Apologies, that's the Chancellor's ring tone. I need to take this."

I made a dismissive gesture. "Don't worry about me, I'll just explore this magnificent building."

She chuckled, then stepped away, answering her call.

I began to wander through the stalls, running fingers over the old hardbacks and relishing the smell of new print.

I didn't discriminate when it came to books —classics or contemporaries, musty tombs or glossy magazines, any form of literature got my heart pounding.

A startled squeak shook me from my book haze, drawing my attention to the rows of desks positioned in the middle of the library common.

"Oh! Shit! Sorry, Dr. Prince! I didn't see you."

A young woman leaped up, turning to apologize to a woman seated on the chair.

"It's quite alright," the seated woman said, brushing her skirts. "Being sat on happens surprisingly often."

The student grimaced. "I saw Jones sit on you at the lecture last week. Maybe you need to wear brighter colors?"

The woman chuckled, the sound surprisingly low and sensual. It flowed slowly through the library like molasses, coating me from top to toe in delicious awareness.

This woman is dangerous.

"I have considered wearing a flashing sign once or twice." She twisted, gathering her things. "Here, you can have my seat. I need to get moving anyway."

I watched her limbs, each an economy of graceful but utilitarian movement. Three large hardbacks, a notepad, and a small laptop were cradled to her chest as she relinquished the seat to the student.

"Thanks, Professor. See you in class."

The woman nodded, a distracted smile on her face as she moved to the stacks, disappearing into their depth with surprising speed.

Before I realized it, I'd begun to move, my feet determined to follow her.

"Henry? Shall we continue?"

The Dean's question stopped me short.

What were you doing?

I shook myself free of whatever malaise had settled over me, amused by my infatuation with the mysterious woman.

You need more sleep, my friend.

"Yes, let's."

And with a last glance behind me, I followed the Dean.

CHAPTER 4

Enid

ENID

More like triple. At least this one
was a student and apologised.

KEIKO

No victim blaming this time?
That's a relief. We should get
you a sign. Or a standing desk.
Or you should quit your job and
become a spy! Yes! If you blend
so well, you'd be next level!

I blew out a sigh my tension easing at Keiko's
teasing.

ENID

Haha...

KEIKO

Have you met him yet?

I didn't need to ask who *he* was.

ENID

Not yet. But he's in the building.

My pulse fluttered, my palms beginning to
sweat.

KEIKO

I looked him up. The man is hot
for an academic. You should
totally get his number.

I snorted, typing out one last message before tossing my phone back in my bag.

ENID

When pigs fly.

I tried to concentrate on revising my lecture notes. I taught four classes a semester on top of my research workload. While most of the faculty managed to negotiate down to three classes to allow more time for research, I kept my full load for two reasons—I loved teaching, and I wanted tenure. Badly. I'd worked here long enough to realize that the Dean loved those who showed the most dedication to their teaching hours.

Manipulation, thy name is Enid.

"Enid! Is that young man arriving today?"

I looked up from my laptop to see Phillip Gordon standing in front of my desk. The old professor had decided to retire at the end of the year after a career that spanned more than four decades. He was well respected, well researched, and an incredible individual. It was because of him that I was where I was.

And it's because of him that I'll get tenure.

Grateful didn't even begin to cover what I felt.

"He is." I glanced at my watch, acting as if I

didn't know the exact time. "Shortly, I should think."

As if on cue, the Dean opened the door to our offices, poking her head inside.

"Is now a good time to introduce Dr. Tenil?"

Phillip chuckled. "We were just talking about him. Come on in, Linda."

She pushed the door open, and I slowly rose, my heart in my throat as Henry Tenil walked through the door.

He's perfect.

A mop of dark hair, a body both lean and muscular, thick glasses that emphasized his flashing green eyes, and a smile a mile wide—Henry was the kind of academic that student-teacher romance books were made of.

I'd let him get between my covers.

I flushed as his gaze met mine, his eyebrow quirking just a touch as if to ask, *Did I hear you correctly?*

"Henry, these are two of our best faculty members, Phillip and Enid."

Henry held out a hand for Phillip to shake. "Pleasure to meet you, sir. Your latest publication on Queer representation in indie publishing was fascinating."

"Well, thank you." Phillip grinned, brushing a hand across his bushy beard. "I spent two years researching that. I'm glad someone read it."

"Oh definitely. Back at King's College it made quite the splash."

Phillip's cheeks flushed red, a modest smile touching his lips. "Well," he murmured, delight clear in his tone. "Well, how 'bout that."

"And Enid." Henry turned to me, his hands clasping mine in both of his. "I've read every one of your works and I must say, I'm fanboying a little right now. If I still pinned pictures on my walls, yours would be front and center."

I stared into the eyes of the man I'd fantasized about for years, my heart pounding out of my chest.

"I... sorry?"

"Your works! Your argument on the influence of post-normative fiction and the need to change the pedagogy was...." He trailed off, shaking his head. "Revolutionary. I'm quite chuffed to meet you."

"I...." I seemed unable to do anything beyond stutter, such was my shock. "Thank you."

"Your desk is over here," Linda said, gently prying Henry away from me, and leading him to the cubicle down from mine. "I'm afraid we're undergoing some major renovations at the moment so we're all tossed in here until they're finished."

"Not a problem," Henry said cheerfully, dropping his bag on his desk. "I'll enjoy being in such close proximity to my heroes."

Phillip sidled up next to me as Linda and Henry continued to chat.

"He's quite the charmer."

I swallowed, unable to pull my gaze away from the captivating man.

"Enid?"

I finally glanced up, giving Phillip a questioning look.

"You should give him your number."

"When pigs fly," I retorted automatically.

Phillip watched me for a minute then grinned, his hands flicking out to his side and flapping a little as he began to walk away.

"Oink, oink."

I glanced back at Henry, finding him with his back to me. My gaze dropped, zeroing in on the most perfect bubble butt I'd ever had the opportunity to behold.

Oink, oink indeed.

CHAPTER 5

Henry

She is magnificent.
Enid commanded the room as she explained the beauty of an unreliable narrator.

"Look at *Rebecca, Fight Club,* and *Gone Girl.* They all work seamlessly to bind the reader to the narrator's truth. But slowly that truth becomes tarnished. It fractures like weight applied to thin ice, corroding as you begin to doubt what you read. Who is right? Who is telling the truth? Why does this character both compel and repel? Where is their moral compass, and how do you lead your readers on a merry trail that slowly but surely forces them to question their own judgment about that character?"

She clicked through her slides, articulating clearly the various ways you could build this kind of storytelling into your work.

"This week I'm asking for a two-page profile on your characters focusing on what makes them unreliable. Even if you're not choosing to employ this technique, no character is always right. I want to see in what ways they're wrong. Think back to our class on motivation and ego and work it in. Alright, see you all next week."

The class broke, but students lingered, chatting animatedly in small groups about their characters, their excitement catching.

Perhaps I should begin plotting my next book.

At the front of the class, there was a short line to speak to Enid. Students mustered around her as she patiently answered questions, discussed techniques, and clarified points.

I began to make my way down to the front of the class, listening intently to her answers.

"Mm, I see what you mean. But, Isabell, you need to bring that ego to life. Play into it, build the tension with your character's words and deeds. We want readers to be sucked into your story. We want them to be hanging on every sentence beat."

The student nodded. "So, I need to rework it."

"Yes. But before you do, go back and learn your characters. They should be singing to you. Demanding how they're written. They should leap from the page with a staff yelling, 'YOU SHALL NOT PASS!'"

The students chuckled.

"Those are the characters people remember. They're the ones with fully formed faces and rich backgrounds. If I say Harry you say?"

"Potter," Isabella said with a laugh, nodding her understanding.

"Very good." Enid made a dismissive gesture. "Now go forth and write."

"Aye, aye, Professor."

A hand tapped my shoulder. I turned, finding a young man staring at me with wide eyes.

"Excuse me, but are you, Henry Tenil?"

I nodded. "That's me."

"Oh my gosh!" The student began to freak out, his skin flushing, his eyes dancing as his hands came up, smashing against his chest as if he were searching for something. "Oh my gosh, I cannot believe this is happening! I love your

Shadow Games series. Professor Prince had us study the series last summer and I fell in love. That scene with Rosa Marie and Gwendolyn, when—"

"Spoilers!" Enid and I yelled at the same time, our heads twisting to stare at each other.

The remaining students fell silent, gazes bouncing from me to Enid and back.

Well, this is interesting.

Enid broke eye contact first. "Sorry, Omar. But what is the first rule of this class?"

The boy grinned. "Don't be a dick."

"And the subclause?"

"No spoilers." He chuckled. "My bad, Prof."

Enid laughed, her face radiant as she grinned at the young man. "Don't worry. I know how it feels."

My gut clenched, a strange, uncomfortable feeling taking root in my belly.

Is that... jealousy? Am I envious that she's sharing her smiles with others?

I filed the question away for further exploration.

"Dr. Tenil will be our guest lecturer at Thursday's class."

Omar gasped, laying hands on his chest. "No way," he breathed, staring at me as if I hung the moon. "This is a dream come true."

Enid grinned. "Dr. Tenil, anything you want to tease before our next class?"

The gathered students leaned in, collectively holding their breaths as they stared at me in rapt attention.

"Love." The word fell from my lips before I'd had a moment to process it. "Love, romance, and the power of attraction."

The students were so quiet I worried I'd alienated them. I glanced at Enid, finding her rich whisky-colored eyes sparkling.

"After all, what is a story without epic love?"

"Shit," Omar muttered, shaking his head. "You sound exactly like the Professor."

Enid's gaze held mine, a small smile playing on her lips.

"And on that note, I must run to my next class." She gathered her equipment, shooting me another of those mysterious smiles. "Coming, Dr. Tenil?"

I nearly stumbled over my feet in my eagerness. "Definitely."

CHAPTER 6

Henry

Enid's next class was just as fascinating as the last, her joy and excitement for the subjects clear for anyone to see.

"And that," she said with a flourish of her hands. "Is the beauty of a satisfactory climax."

The class tittered at the terminology but I saw more than half of them jot down notes.

"Now, I don't have time for questions this afternoon—I'm afraid we've run over." Her gaze met mine, amusement curving her lips into a small smile. "And our Fellowship Researcher, Henry Tenil, is rather desperate to begin trawling through our trove of ancient texts. But, as always, you can email me any questions and my office hours are two-to-five on Fridays." She paused, her gaze still on me.

"Class dismissed."

Unlike their senior counterparts, the majority of the freshmen surged from their seats rushing to escape the classroom leaving only the die-hard literary fanatics behind. Of these, some I could tell were here for what they assumed was an easy pass. Some were here for enjoyment. But, and they were rare and hard to identify, a select few would be the ones most likely to follow this path.

Librarians, readers, or writers. It matters not when we are bound together by words and imagination.

I captured the thought, mulling it over as I made my way to Enid's side.

"Ready?" she asked, reaching for her laptop bag.

"Allow me." I snatched the strap, looping it over my shoulder before gesturing at her to precede me.

Out in the sunshine, we made our way through the campus in companionable silence, the tension building between us.

I wonder what she tastes like.

The woman beside me glanced up, shooting me a shy grin. "Are you enjoying Ravenburn so far?"

I nodded. "Very much."

"I can't imagine it compares to home though."

"I wouldn't say that." I gave her what I hoped was a flirty wink. "The professors are certainly more attractive."

Enid's face flushed, her head dropping as hair covered her red cheeks.

"Th-th-the entry to the rare books collection is this way."

She led me down a small alley, showing me the non-descript door.

"Swipe access only. We'll organize that for you tomorrow."

She shoved the door open, lights beginning to flick on as a sensor picked up our movement.

"Oh," I murmured, shuffling to a stop. "Wow."

Long rows of shelving were interspaced with climate-controlled display cabinets. Books older than the Mayflower were housed in the clear displays, their precious pages perfectly preserved.

"That was my reaction too," Enid said with a laugh, beginning to walk across the room. "I hope you don't mind, but I pulled all of Cedric's works from storage. I've set you up back here at one of our research tables."

I followed her through the space, my body

tense with anticipation as we moved to the research area. On a long table were piles and piles of old, worn hardbacks. The leather-bound volumes were carefully stacked, a pair of soft white gloves resting beside them.

I placed Enid's laptop bag and my backpack on a chair, reaching for the gloves.

"These are all of Cedric's books," Enid explained, gesturing at the numerous titles. "But in the storage boxes you'll find the entire contents of Miss Steinbeck's estate relating to Cedric. It includes letters and diary entries and all manner of things." She grinned, tapping a box with one finger. "Miss Steinbeck was a hoarder, which means a lot of these items haven't been processed yet. You may find some unpublished works in amongst the gossip."

"I can only hope."

We both laughed then Enid stepped away from the table.

"I should leave you to it. No doubt you're dying to get started."

"Wait. Why don't you stay?" I gestured at the storage tubs. "This will take me weeks but between the two of us we might be able to process it all a little quicker."

Enid's impossibly large eyes grew wider.

"M-m-me?" she asked, pointing at herself. "You want my assistance?"

I nodded. "There's nothing I'd love more."

"But... why?"

Because I've been a massive fan of your work for years? Because I find you more intriguing every moment I spend with you? Because you're a stunning beauty and I cannot stop looking at you?

"Because I need the help."

The words felt woefully inadequate and inaccurate. But it was what I said in an effort to keep her near.

Enid bit her lower lip, a small frown marring her brow as she considered my request.

"We could co-write the paper," I offered, attempting to sweeten the deal. "And, if we prove my theory, we can share the credit."

Enid laughed, shaking her head. "You think I'm a fame-chaser?"

"No. But I know you Astipian's like to brag about the various papers you've published."

She grinned, her eyes dancing. "That we do." Enid stuck her hand out for me to shake. "Alright. You have a deal."

I took her hand, our palms pressing together, our fingers tight and warm as we shook on it.

"Deal," I repeated.

For a moment our gazes lingered, our hands

resting together as something new and exciting bounced between us.

Enid broke eye contact first.

"Shall we get to work?" she asked, dropping my hand and turning away.

For a minute I wanted to reach out and pull her back into me. I wanted to press our palms and entwine our fingers together while I kissed her senseless.

My cock pressed against my fly, my body throbbing as I stared at her back.

"Henry?" she asked, glancing over her shoulder as she pulled on gloves. "Are you ready to work now?"

I cleared my throat.

"Yeah, let's get started."

CHAPTER 7

Phillip stood at my desk staring at me.

"Can I help you?" I asked, cocking one eyebrow in question.

"It's after six on a Friday."

"And?"

The man shook his head. "Why are you still here?"

"Because I'm a boring individual with no love life, or social life, and have already watched all the period dramas available on Netflix."

Behind me, Henry chuckled.

"You two should go out. You're both young, attractive people. Go into town. Get a burger.

Get drunk. Cause some chaos. Live!" Phillip raised his fist, shaking it at the heavens.

"I don't know." Henry tapped the hardback on his desk, shooting me a wink. "I think I'm fully booked."

"You, sir." Phillip waggled a finger in his direction. "Are a pun master and I appreciate it. But seriously kids, go out. Live a little. Make mistakes. Have regrets. Build memories. There's more to life than books and work."

"Is there?" I laughed, sitting back in my chair. "Because when one does what they love for a living is it work?"

"It is." Phillip reached for his bag, shrugging it over his shoulder. "I am off to kiss my husband and say hello to the children before we engage in some hot and heavy rounds of chess while we devour whatever new concoction Edward has designed. I hope your evening is equally as—as the children say—lit."

He turned, tossing his final comment over his shoulder as he strode from the office.

"And, just to say, it's sad when a man of sixty years is living a fuller life than you."

I shook my head as he pulled the door shut, leaving Henry and me in the office.

"You know," Henry said after a beat. "He's right. And it *is* after six. Could I interest you in a dinner date?"

My body froze.

"A-a-a date? With me?"

He laughed, nodding. "Yes, Enid. A date with you. Though it can be a platonic date, should you prefer. Whatever makes you most comfortable." He dropped his voice. "Though I must admit that I'm suffering terribly after nursing an unrequited crush on you for the past few years."

"Me?" I squeaked, seeming unable to participate in this conversation beyond the barest of replies. An unfortunately common experience around Henry.

"Of course, you. Don't you realize how incredible you are? You're the reason I applied for the Fellowship here. Well, that and Cedric of course."

"Of course," I said with a laugh.

"But it was your Ted Talk two years ago on non-binary representation that really hit me. The entire discussion was simultaneously moving and informative, and delivered with such sensitivity and caring that I've been a borderline stalker ever since."

I gaped at him, unable to believe a man who looked like Henry—honestly, he looked like a nerdy Henry Cavil had a baby with a Hemsworth and they raised him to have the awkward adorableness of Topher Grace—

could ever be interested in a bluestocking like me.

"My cousin Dylan is non-binary. I wanted to show that there is importance in representation. They helped me design that talk."

"It was powerful." He cocked his head to one side. "So, dinner?"

"Dinner would be wonderful." I started, unable to believe those words had slipped out of my mouth. "I mean—that is, I—"

"Wonderful! I've heard that the Bronze Horseman is good. Have you been there?"

"Um, yes. A few times. It's very good."

"Great, shall we go?" Henry stood, gathering his things.

"Now?"

"Sure, unless you have something to finish?"

I glanced at my application, the one I'd been tinkering with for the last three days. The submit button sat glaring at me from the computer screen, taunting me to hit it.

"Um, no. Now is good." I hesitated for a moment then hit submit before I could think better of it.

And now I wait.

"Ready?"

Not at all.

"Definitely."

———

We were settled in a booth, the waitress quickly taking our order.

"Be right back with your drinks," she promised, slipping away.

I knit my hands awkwardly in front of me, wondering how people did this regularly.

When was the last time I had dinner with a man I wasn't related to and who wasn't Phillip? Three years ago? No, it must be five. It was that banker from Toronto who kept calling me Edna.

"This is a nice place," Henry said, looking around. "I wonder if it was named for something."

"The owner's last name is Bronze. I think Horseman comes from a joke with her co-owner."

Henry blinked. "How do you know that?"

"Capricorn Cove is a small town. I grew up here. My cousin is married to the chef's sister's best friend."

Henry blinked, processing that. "Your cousin, Dylan?"

I laughed, shaking my head. "No, this is a cousin on my father's side. Caleb, he's a local detective. We're all rather interconnected here."

"Was it fun growing up in a small town?"

"Not at all." I chuckled as our waitress returned, sliding drinks onto the table. "Thanks Emily."

"No problem." The woman dusted her hands on her apron. "You coming to the concert night next week?" she asked

"I'll definitely try."

She nodded then left us alone, Henry shooting me a grin.

"See? Small town."

"It seems delightful."

"It's not. It sucked. Everyone knows your business and once you're labeled as something it's almost impossible to be seen as something different."

"This fascinates me," Henry said, leaning forward. "The idea that growth is not possible."

"It's not *impossible*, it just... isn't common. You really have to do something so fundamentally different that you become someone else in everyone's mind." I shrugged.

"What was your label growing up?"

I chuckled. "Can't you tell?"

"Hmm, most popular?"

"Absolutely not." I flicked my fingers at him. " Geek, nerd, girl with perpetually long list of to-be-reads. I liked to wear black and quote classics."

He chuckled. "I can see it. How about me?"

I narrowed my eyes on him. "Debate club president."

"We don't have debate club where I come from, but I did get elected head boy of my school."

"Of course, you did. You're a charismatic guy."

Henry laughed. "I'm not so sure about that. But I'll accept the compliment."

We talked over burgers, sharing sides and anecdotes about mutual acquaintances in the academic world. For the first time in forever, I felt no reason to make an excuse and politely return home.

"Shall we walk along the marina?" Henry asked when we finally left, his head tilted back to look up at the sky. "It's a beautiful night."

My heart began to hammer in my chest, butterflies fluttering in my stomach.

"Um... sure."

We walked down the street to the long wooden boardwalk, beginning the stroll at the pier.

"Why did you come back?" Henry asked as we slowly walked, pausing here and there to admire the moon as it danced on the water.

"Hmm?"

He made a broad gesture. "This town. You said growing up here sucked. Why come back?"

"Because growing up here sucked. But growing old here doesn't. I left to go to college thinking I'd never return." I laughed, shaking my head. "I transferred to Ravenburn after my second year. I missed being part of a community where people had your back."

I gestured at the water. "And this, of course. Who wouldn't want to live close to this?"

Henry paused, leaning his forearms against the banisters that ran the length of the marina.

"It is beautiful. Stunningly so. I could see myself living here."

My heart skipped. "Really?"

"Certainly. The university—sorry, college— is excellent, the town is friendly, and I'd have meaningful work."

We fell into companionable silence; our bodies close enough that I could feel the heat from his warming my skin.

I found myself staring at his lips, my body beginning to sway closer.

I want to kiss him.

"Enid?"

"Yes?"

"I'm not going to kiss you right now."

My stomach clenched, surprised at how disappointed I felt.

"I understand." I began to withdraw.

"No." He caught my hand. "What I mean is, I want to kiss you. I want it more than anything. But our first kiss has to be perfect, Enid. And my breath smells like garlic."

I bit my lip, a thrill warming my blood. "I like garlic."

He grinned, his teeth flashing in the night. "Noted. But I'm not going to ruin the taste of you with garlic. When we kiss—and note I said when, not if—it will be perfect. I promise."

Later that night, in the dark of my bedroom I savored those words, delighting in his confidence.

It will be perfect. I promise.

CHAPTER 8

Enid

I stared at myself in the mirror pinching the material gathered at my waist.

"And you like this guy?" Keiko asked from her position on my bed.

Yes. I want to ride him like a pony.

For the last few weeks, I'd spent nearly every waking moment with Henry. I'd breathed the same air he'd breathed. I'd eaten the same lunch he'd eaten. I'd read passages and shared thoughts, and every single minute I was with him I could feel that school girl crush melt away to reveal something deeper, stronger, more real.

And he still hasn't kissed me. The waiting is the sweetest kind of torture.

"He's... nice," I said finally.

"Nice?" Keiko sat up. "Nice? Nice as in...?"

"Nice?"

She threw a pillow at my head.

"Nice isn't a word you use for men. Nice is a nothing word. It's a word you use when someone asks if you like their horrendous new artwork. Tell me about how he acts. Tell me about how he makes you *feel*." She clutched at her heart, pretending to fall off the bed as she spasmed.

I rolled my eyes. "If that's your impression of an orgasm, it's no wonder you're a hit 'em and quit 'em kind of woman."

"Hey! I take offense to that comment!" Kei sat up shooting me a narrowed-eyed mock-glare. "There was that one guy."

"Mm." I tried not to laugh. "Are we talking about the man you forgot you'd taken to bed?"

"In my defense, he'd changed. A lot."

"Steroids will do that to you."

She sighed noisily. "Yeah. Such a shame too. I hate when the charisma doesn't match the package. It's like empty calories—a complete waste of a meal."

I snorted, turning back to the mirror.

"This looks frumpy, doesn't it?"

"Do you want the truth or the nice?"

I laughed, giving her the finger. "Go on then."

"Frumpy AF. Girl, you need to work your body." She tilted her head to one side, her curtain of dark hair falling over her shoulder. "Who are you trying to impress? Yourself, Henry, or the Dean?"

"Which answer will get you to help me?"

She laughed, leaping off the bed. "Any, but the answer will depend on how daring we go."

"If I say myself, what are we thinking?"

"Babe. Trust me. I got you."

The outfit she settled on wasn't what I'd wear. It wasn't even *close* to anything I'd wear. But Keiko had pulled the paisley print dress from the depth of my closet, pinned it and quickly hemmed it, then added accessories, ankle boots, and gently curled the bottom of my hair until I looked like a Hallmark movie heroine going to a cookout.

"I look ridiculous."

"You look hot."

"I feel like a cowgirl."

"Well, go find a nice cock to ride."

I burst out laughing, rolling my eyes at Keiko in the mirror. "Thank you."

She grinned. "You're welcome. Now go get your man and your promotion!"

———

The welcome mixer held the usual suspects. The upper echelons of the College mingled in the center of the room, surrounded by talented, gregarious professors, and aspiring researchers. In a surprise to no one, Phillip and I had found a little corner of the room and were safely ensconced far away from the main rabble.

"But why? Why must we unmask these authors?" Phillip asked, shaking his head. "If they wrote under a pen name then it must be for a reason. It seems to me that people for whom unmasking an author is a badge of pride aren't doing so for transparency, but rather with malicious intent."

I stiffened as Henry slid into our conversation.

"Enid, Phillip, hello. Sorry to interrupt but I couldn't help but overhear. Is this in relation to the George Oliver report?"

The hair on my arms prickled as Henry sidled closer, slipping easily into our intimate space.

Why does he have to be so attractive? Why did he promise to kiss me? Why do I care so much?

"Indeed," Phillip said, shifting to make

room for the Brit. "Enid and I are just discussing the ethics of revealing a pen name."

Henry glanced my way, his gaze appreciative as he looked me over. "That's a lovely outfit, Enid."

My cheeks warmed, my gaze dropping to his shoes. "Thank you. You look rather lovely too."

Oh, God. Did I really just say that?

Henry chuckled, the sound deep, genuine, and joyful.

"And me?" Phillip asked, shooting his arms out straight from his sides. "What about me? Am I lovely too?"

"Always," I said with a grin.

"Brilliant. Now, back to the subject at hand," Phillip said, arms dropping back to his sides. "The unmasking of the artist."

"Amateur sleuths seeking fame?" I suggested, sipping at my tepid soda.

"More like headhunters," Phillip muttered, shaking his head. "These are people seeking fame and fortune by revealing a piece of someone that isn't theirs. It's hurtful. And harmful."

Henry tilted his head to one side. "I agree—to a point."

My eyebrows rose in surprise.

"My research on Cedric Cagle has the

potential to reveal that Cedric may be a woman. Cedric wrote in a time when women were not taken seriously, not believed to be free thinkers capable of influence. I believe, if Cedric really is Mary, then she deserves to be celebrated."

Phillip and I exchanged a look.

"And who are you, young man, to unearth such a woman? Who are you to strip back the mask, the persona this person worked so hard to build?"

Henry blinked then blinked again. "I... no one, I suppose."

"Then why would you want to reveal that which the author did not?"

Henry seemed lost for words.

I reached over, giving his arm a squeeze. "Don't worry, Phillip likes to play devil's advocate."

The older man chuckled, his great belly bouncing with his merriment. "That I do. But the question stands."

"But what," I countered, unable to stop myself from coming to Henry's defense. "What if she had wanted herself to be revealed but lacked the opportunity?"

Phillip shrugged. "Until I could see it in her own words, I'd have to believe that the woman—what did you say her name was?"

"Mary Allen."

"Right. I'd have to believe that Ms. Allen wanted nothing more than to have privacy."

Henry looked crestfallen. "So, you're saying my life's work is nothing but a head-hunting mission?"

Phillip shrugged. "I'm saying it depends on what Mary herself says. You have a veritable library of resources from which to draw. Surely something in that heap of gossip paper and plot holes will reveal her true self."

Henry sucked in a breath, his lips quirking into a wry smile. "Well, I certainly hope so. Otherwise, I'm afraid this junket has been for naught—research-wise at least." His gaze slid to me, his grin quick and easy. "Listening to even one of Enid's passionate lectures is enough to have made this worthwhile."

My cheeks—already flushed—warmed further. My face felt as if it radiated enough heat to burn the building down.

"Dr. Prince, a word?"

I turned, finding the Dean standing nearby.

"Of course." I turned back to Phillip and Henry. "Excuse me."

With a quick step, I followed Linda out into the lobby.

"Is something wrong?" I asked, not liking the little furrow marring Linda's brow.

"No, it's just...." She paused, crossing her arms over her chest. "As you would be aware, Phillip is retiring at the end of the year."

My body went damp, nervous sweat immediately breaking out as my anxiety ratcheted up.

"Yes, I'm aware."

Linda's lips pursed together as she watched me for a long moment.

"And you've applied."

"I have."

Her frown deepening. "And you're absolutely set on this course?"

I nodded; my tongue too thick in my mouth to answer.

"Hmm." She tapped one foot against the ground. "Alright, thank you for your time."

And with that, she turned on her heel, heading back into the crowded great room, leaving me in stunned uncertainty.

What the fuck was that?

"Enid?"

I jumped, my heart about leaping through my chest.

"Henry!" I swore, shaking my head. "You scared me."

"Apologies," he said, sheepishly. "I just wanted to check if anything was amiss."

I loved the way he spoke, intersecting old-fashioned verbiage with modern phrases. There was something wholesome about him, even as he gave off an 'I'll-meet-your-father-if-you-call-me-Daddy' vibe.

"I'm okay," I said, dropping my gaze to the floor. "The Dean just wanted to talk shop."

"Why do you do that?"

"Do what?"

"Look at my toes? Am I scary?"

I forced myself to lift my head. "No. I'm sorry. It's just that you make me nervous. Sorry."

"Is it because of the kiss?"

I shook my head. "No, just... sorry."

"You don't need to be sorry or nervous. Just try to do better."

I blinked. "Excuse me?"

"Do better," Henry repeated, reaching out to run the back of his knuckles against my cheek. "Because if you do better at meeting people's gaze, then you'll gift the world with your gorgeous eyes."

Wait. Hold up. What is happening right now?

"Um...." Words failed me.

With a small knowing grin, Henry stepped forward slowly, his body breaching my personal space.

"And those gorgeous eyes lead one to see

your magnificent lips," he said, his voice low. "And when I see them there's nothing I want more than to...." He trailed off, his thumb brushing over my mouth.

"Than?" I asked, my voice soft even as my body throbbed with need.

"Than to kiss you." He leaned down, his words dancing across my lips like a caress. "Let me kiss you, Enid. I've been craving a taste since we first met, and now is the perfect time."

Is this really happening?

In a moment that I was sure had been plucked from a romance novel or perhaps a movie I'd once watched, Henry leaned in, catching my lips in a devastating kiss.

Oh, dear.

CHAPTER 9

Henry

I'm not sure what had come over me. Perhaps it was the uncertainty on Enid's face after she'd spoken to the Dean. Maybe it had been the fall of hair over her beautiful face that had set me off. Or perhaps it was the outfit she wore that suited her so well.

I'd planned to kiss her over dinner and wine. I'd planned a romantic night of literature and laughs—not after a discussion where she defended my life's work.

But her doing so had broken a need free within me, demanding I claim this woman.

Don't let her get away.

There was something magical about Enid. A spark that burned bright. She was the most beautiful woman in every room, her eyes flashing, her smile wide and welcoming. But if I gave her even the smallest amount of attention that spark disappeared, hidden behind a veil of uncertainty.

She reminded me of the squiggles you occasionally saw in the corners of your eyes—if you tried to focus on them, they'd dart away, disappearing as if never there.

I deepened our kiss, pulling her closer, pressing my body against hers. Everything about this felt right—Enid pressed against me, the taste of her, the feel of her in my arms.

Then I drew back, slowly and with great reluctance, but knowing she needed time and space to process our kiss. Knowing I needed to give her the space to choose me.

Fuck. It's hard being a good person.

I leaned my forehead against hers, savoring the taste of her on my tongue.

"Enid?"

"Yes?"

I lifted her chin, ensuring our gazes caught, giving her no room to escape me.

"Just so you're fully aware, I wanted that. I want more of you. I want all your kisses. I want all your attention." I sucked in a breath. "I might be more than a little infatuated with you."

She blinked, her eyes wide and uncertain.

"I... really?"

"Oh yes." I pressed a kiss to her lips. "I'll apologize for rushing this, but I won't apologize for that kiss."

Her cheeks flushed her gaze dropping.

"No, don't look away, give me your gaze."

She slowly looked up.

"There you are. Please don't hide from me, Enid. Your eyes are far too beautiful and expressive to be hidden."

She seemed lost for words.

With a resigned sigh, I stepped back, knowing we needed to return to the great room before any tongues began to wag.

"We should get back."

She nodded and began to move towards the doors, stopping when I didn't follow.

"Are you coming?"

I huffed out a laugh, looking pointedly at my erection. "I need a moment."

Or five hundred.

She bit her lip, her gaze trained on my crotch.

"Shit," I muttered, my body heating. "Don't do this to me, Enid. I may be an incredible academic but I'm only a man."

A giggle burst free, that magical spark catching.

"I'll see you in there. I'll be the wallflower standing beside the jolly Santa."

She pulled the door open and disappeared inside before I could tell her how ridiculous her description of herself was.

"You are no wallflower, my Enid-love. You're an exotic hothouse bloom just waiting to unfurl."

CHAPTER 10

Enid

I paused in the doorway of the research lab with two cups of coffee in my hands, watching as Henry gently turned the pages of the old books, his gaze rapt as he read the book of prose by Cedric.

"Sorry to interrupt," I said, coming over to set a cup by his desk. "But we need to finish up here if we're going to get to your class soon."

Henry pulled back, pushing his glasses up to rub the bridge of his nose. "Thank you for the reminder." He tapped the pages of the book. "I'm ready to get lost in this literary masterpiece for days."

I took a sip, savoring the coffee. "What's this poem about?"

"How about I read it to you?"

He lifted the book, his smooth, crisp voice reciting the prose.

> *"She is no beauty, no wailing song*
> *She is like the timeless mountains*
> *The ranges and rivers where they run*
> *She is a light dotted sky*
> *Ever lasting*
> *Ever living*
> *Ever loved."*

I sighed dreamily. "That was beautiful."

"Like you."

I forced myself to meet his gaze, finding it warm.

He's going to kiss me.

Sure enough, he came to me, pressing a light kiss to my lips.

"Hello, Enid."

"Hello, Henry."

"Thank you for the coffee."

"Thank you for the kisses."

He grinned, stepping back. "My absolute pleasure."

After taking a fortifying sip of my coffee, I

gestured at the books. "Do you really think Cedric is a woman?"

"I not only think that, I believe that Mary Allen was in love with a woman."

I raised my eyebrows. "Really?"

"Yes." He reached for his notebook, flipping through.

"Here, there are letters from Cedric to a Mrs. Myer. The woman references Sarah James. She says, '*And tell me about Sarah James. Does she treat you well? You've been living together these last two years and I must have it on your authority that she is worthy of you. Write me soon.*'"

Henry looked up, his grin wide. "I think they were lovers."

My heart did a little pitter-patter at the thought. "I hope they had a wonderful life together."

My phone beeped, letting me know we'd reached our deadline.

"Come on, class awaits."

———

It was standing room only for Henry's lecture. As the author of multiple bestsellers, and a series that had its own cult following, Henry was a big name in a small school. It made sense that everyone from the Chancellor down was in attendance.

"Love," Henry began as the audience quieted. "Is a splendid thing. It's a soul meeting a soul on a lover's lips. There is no charm equal to tenderness of heart."

He paused, grinning. "These quotes come from literature older than this school. They come from people long dead. And yet they resonate with us. Why? What is it about love that makes men destroy cities, and women sacrifice all? And why is it that we love to read about this delightfully human emotion?"

His gaze met mine. "Let's explore love together, shall we?"

Over the next two hours, Henry dissected the emotion with the skill of a surgeon. He talked about the power of love, the fear of it, the magnitude. He discussed the importance of a love story and the connection that two characters could feel.

And he made me fall in love with him.

I wanted to resist. I wanted to stop this crazy feeling from dragging me under. I wanted to hit pause on him and all that he represented. But the man had a point.

"Love is love. And we humans love it. Thank you."

The auditorium exploded with applause,

the spell he'd woven around us shattering as we were swept back from the brink of love to crash into the reality of life.

He's a storyteller.

"Well, that was quite the lecture," Phillip said, shaking his head. "Do you think he does something like that every time he speaks?"

"I hope so."

As the crowd began to filter out, I hovered near the stage, waiting for the man who'd begun to burrow into my heart.

It's too soon. It's far too soon, Enid. You know better.

Henry's words came back to me. "The heart knows what it wants."

"Henry!" The Dean strode across the stage, her hands clasping his and shaking vigorously. "A truly excellent lecture. I can't tell you how long it's been since we had such a turnout."

"Thank you, Linda. It was an absolute privilege to speak at your school."

She brushed him off with a dismissive little wave. "Psh, you're too kind." She leaned in, and the next words out of her mouth broke my heart.

"Have you thought about applying for Phillip's position? We'd love to have you."

I froze, my body turning to stone as Linda waited for Henry's reply. Beside me, Phillip stiffened, his hand reaching out to wrap around my arm.

"Stay here?" Henry's head turned, his gaze meeting mine. A slow smile spread across his face. "Well, now that you mention it, I hadn't but if it means I could remain at Ravenburn then maybe it's something to think about."

"Do," Linda told him, giving his hands one last shake. "I expect you'll be a key candidate."

And with that she turned, striding out of the auditorium, leaving behind the ragged debris that was the remains of my life.

CHAPTER 11

Enid

Later that week I lay on my bed, face pressed into my pillow as Keiko paced, wearing a hole in the carpet.

"I'll kill her," she threatened angrily. "Or him. No, I'll kill them both."

"Don't," I said into the pillow. "It's not worth a life sentence."

Kei scoffed. "Honey, you're worth *multiple* life sentences."

I laughed, pushing myself up to a seat. "I appreciate the sentiment, but the world would be a sadder place without you free to unleash your amazing self on the world."

Keiko nodded. "It's true. I am amazing."

I rolled my eyes.

"But that doesn't mean these bastards shouldn't be held accountable. They can't take that job away from you, Enid. You've worked too hard for too long to allow that to happen."

I blew out a breath. "But the thing is, they can. If the Dean thinks Henry's a better fit, then why wouldn't she award him the position? It's not as if he isn't qualified."

"Just because something is true, doesn't mean it's right."

I shook my head. "In this instance, truth and righteousness are interwoven. It sucks, but I'm not going to lie to myself. Henry has every reason to apply and every reason to get it."

"Then you know what you have to do."

I cocked an eyebrow in question.

"Get stabby." Keiko lifted a clenched fist making a stabbing motion.

"Jesus, Kei. No. I'm not going to kill anyone. This isn't a crime novel."

But it's not shaping up to be a romance, either. Unfortunately.

The fact was, as much as I wished to be with Henry—and as delicious as his kisses had been—I knew if he won Phillip's position then I'd become resentful of him. I'd feel inferior and I'd question what he had that I didn't. I'd obsess about what I could have done differently, and constantly be concerned that people would view me as nothing but an accessory to a successful man.

I'm human enough to admit that it would break me.

"Then what are you going to do?"

"Nothing."

"What?" Kei stared at me. "What do you mean nothing? Not even speak to Mister-Delicious-Kisses?"

I hesitated.

"No."

"Why the fuck not?"

"Because I don't want to prejudice his decision. Henry's made it more than clear he's interested in me, to think that I would use that to sway his future is reprehensible."

Kei shook her head. "I think you're making a mistake."

"I know. And it could be, but right now this is the only decision I'm comfortable with."

She reached out, clasping my hand. "This sucks ass."

I huffed out a sad laugh. "Yeah, it does."

"What are you going to do? Will you keep seeing him?"

And there's the million-dollar question.

I still didn't understand what he saw in me. Henry, a man who looked like a movie star and had the voice of a romance hero, claimed I was magnificent. He said I sparkled. He said my eyes were beautiful, and I reminded him of spun silk and rich spices. He treated me with kindness and respect, actually listening to what I had to say.

I hated that he was so easy to love.

"This would be so much easier if he was a dick."

Kei laughed. "So that's a yes?"

I bit my lip, giving over to my feelings.

"Yes."

The decision was both the easiest and hardest I'd ever made.

As if I'd summoned him, my phone rang, Henry's name flashing on the screen.

"Enid love, come to dinner with me."

I closed my eyes, enjoying the way his voice felt like a sweet caress.

"It's a school night," I said, teasing.

"Then we'll stay in. I'll cook."

"You cook?"

"Well, I'll try."

I laughed, delighted by his honesty. "How about you organize dessert and I'll cook?"

"Sounds like a plan." His voice dropped,

his tone rough. "But I'm not sure I'll need dessert when I have your sweet mouth to taste."

My body shivered, delicious spirals of needy heat slowly spinning through my body.

"Henry...."

He chuckled. "Until tonight, Enid love."

I hung up, staring at the blank screen for a long moment.

"You're in trouble," Kei said sagely.

"Yep."

"Do you love him?"

"It's too soon for love."

Kei laughed, pushing off the bed to stand, her arms raising over her head as she stretched.

"Too soon for love? Never. What is the point of all those romance novels if not to prove that love is the only thing that matters?"

She tilted her head to one side. "Don't underestimate your ability to love someone, Enid. You are capable of so much more than you think. And the man you love? He'll be a fucking lucky man. You deserve only the best, my friend."

She dropped her arms, giving a sassy little shimmer. "Now, I'll see you tomorrow."

"Are you going out?" I asked, watching her sashay to the doorway.

"No, but you are."

With a wink, she walked out then poked her head back in my room.

"Oh, and wear some cute underwear. Maybe the green—you'll look hot as fuck."

With that piece of advice, my housemate left me alone to contemplate ego, love, romance, and matching underwear.

CHAPTER 12

Henry

"I need help."

Kat, my sister, laughed down the phone line.

"You always need help. What kind of help are we talking?"

"The kind that involves impressing someone."

Kat was silent for a beat. "Hold on, let me get Hayden."

"I don't need—"

"Hayden! My brother requires assistance!"

I heard a dog barking in the background then a clatter as my sister's boyfriend made his presence known.

"Henry! How are you? Dude, are we still on for that surfing trip? I'm dying for a break."

"Yep," I said, grinning at his enthusiasm. "I've already hired a board."

"Excellent."

Hayden and my sister had fallen in love over the summer while we'd been visiting my aunt. I couldn't think of a better man for Kat. My sister was a prickly individual, full of heat and fire. Whereas Hayden tempered her, adding water until all that was left was the steam between them.

"Henry wants to impress a woman."

"A local woman?" Hayden asked Kat.

"I think so."

"She is," I confirmed, pinching the bridge of my nose.

This is what I get for asking for help.

"And who is she?"

"Oh! Can I guess?" Kat said, laughing down the phone line.

"Go on then," I sighed, resigned to my fate.

"Enid Prince." Kat's voice was frustratingly smug. "She's the one who you bookmarked on YouTube. Hayden, I have to tell you, my brother rarely looks at women. He's practically a monk. And yet this Enid? He had alerts set up so he gets an email if articles reference her."

"Naww, your bro has a fan-crush."

Lord, if you're listening, now would be a good time to strike me down.

"Am I right?" Kat asked, her tone knowing.

I blew out a breath. "Unfortunately, yes."

"Ha! Told you! Now, tell us what you need."

"I'm not sure I care anymore," I admitted. "You've quite put me off."

"Shut up and spill," Kat barked.

I blew out a breath. "Enid is *the* woman. And she is coming over tonight for dinner."

"Have you kissed?" Kat demanded. "Please tell me you've kissed her."

"A gentleman never kisses and tells."

"He has," Kat told Hayden. "He'd have said no if they didn't."

"Sometimes I really question why I didn't smother you in your sleep," I grumbled.

She cackled. "Because you loooooooovvvvve me."

"I do, but that doesn't mean you're not frustrating and completely annoying."

Both of them chuckled.

"So, you have this Enid coming over for dinner. What are you ordering?" Hayden asked.

My cooking disasters were family legends.

"I'm attempting to make a dessert."

There was a beat of silence.

"Is the fire brigade on standby?" Kat asked.

"Do you have life insurance?" Hayden followed up.

"Surely not killing your date is a good option."

"Did you warn her about possible food poisoning?"

"Let me order something for you," Kat offered. "What's your new address?"

"I don't need your criticism," I told them sternly. "I need your assistance."

"What are you planning?" Kat asked.

"Brownies."

There was a long pause on the other end of the phone.

"Oh, for fuck's sake," I snapped. "What?"

"How about," Hayden suggested. "I send you a brownie in a cup recipe? It's microwaveable which means you can't stuff it up."

"Don't underestimate the power of the devil," my horrible sibling muttered.

I made a sound. "Yes, Hayden-who-is-now-my-favourite. I would adore your recipe."

"In the divorce, you'll be stuck with me," my sister warned.

"In the divorce, I choose the person willing to help me win my wife."

There was a beat of silence on the other end of the phone.

"Wife?" Kat whispered.

Damn.

"Well, not yet. Obviously. But I have high hopes."

"Wow... this is...." Kat trailed off.

"You can't say fast, you and Hayden were fast. I mean you've known each other for less than a few months and you're already living together."

"Fine. Unexpected then." I could practically hear Kat's eye roll down the phone.

"Unexpected doesn't mean it isn't welcome," Hayden said, his voice soft. "Sometimes you just know."

There was a pause as we all processed his statement.

"Alright, I'll send you the recipe now. You need anything else?" Hayden asked.

"No, I'm good."

"Have a great night, brother." Kat made kissy sounds down the phone line. "Don't do anything I wouldn't!"

"Or do! Your sister is actually quite boring."

There was a sound of outrage before the phone went dead.

The doorbell rang, my body stiffening in anticipation.

Enid.

"Hey you're early—" I broke off as I yanked the door open, finding the Dean standing on my porch.

"Linda? I mean, this is unexpected. Can I help you?"

"Do you have a moment?" she asked, her expression unreadable.

No. I'm expecting my future wife at any moment.

"Sure, come on in."

I glanced out at the street, finding it empty.

Damn. I really hope Enid arrives soon.

The last thing I wanted was to spend my night talking about work.

"Would you like a drink?" I asked, guiding her into the sitting room.

"No, I'm fine. But you should sit."

I hesitated then took the armchair, settling across from her.

"Is something wrong?"

She considered me for a moment then nodded as if confirming a decision.

"Henry, I'd like to offer you the tenured position."

I blinked.

"I'm sorry, what?"

"Phillip is retiring and we have a vacancy

fast approaching. You're young, talented, and a drawcard for donors. We want you."

"I... I'm not sure what to say."

"Say yes. Say you'll accept."

I thought of Enid, of the opportunity this gave us to be together beyond my Fellowship.

"Yes. A hundred percent, yes."

CHAPTER 13

Enid

I arrived at Henry's town house, a grocery bag in hand.

"Welcome," he said, practically vibrating with energy. "Come in, come in!"

I laughed at his enthusiasm, delighted by the exuberant kisses he pressed against my lips.

"You're in a good mood."

"I am. It's been the kind of day where dreams come true."

He took the bag from me, leading me into the kitchen.

"Dreams, hey? Did you find a letter declaring Cedric is Mary?"

He snorted. "That would be the icing on an already delicious cake. Alas, no. But I have hopes that...." He continued to talk as I watched him move around the kitchen.

There was something about him being in his home, about the way he occupied the space but invited me to be a part of it that got my engine running.

My fingers went to the buttons on the front of my dress, beginning to slip them free.

Am I really doing this?

It appeared I was.

"...and then Linda stopped by and—" Henry froze, cutting himself off as he turned to me, a bushel of parsley in his hand.

"Enid."

My name fell from his lips like a prayer.

Oh, I like that.

I shrugged off my dress, letting it pool at my feet.

"Enid."

Henry moved, coming to stand before me, his hands reaching out but hovering above my skin. Goose bumps rose as I waited for him to touch me.

"I don't know where to start," he admitted, his gaze dancing over every curve of my body. "I feel like a starved man and you're a feast I can't wait to sample."

"And yet you're not." I moved closer, using

the last of my courage to lay a hand on his chest. "Touch me, Henry."

He shifted, his hands falling to my waist as he backed me up, pressing me against a wall.

"I'm going to kiss every inch of your beautiful body." His rasped promise raised goose bumps across my skin.

Yes, please.

I licked my lips, acutely aware of the throbbing pulse of desire pooling in my lower abdomen.

"Well, do it."

He grinned, then leaned in, capturing my lips with his, his tongue slipping in to dance with mine.

It wasn't a soft kiss or one of slow exploration. This was heat, and passion, and claiming, possessive need. He kissed me as if I were made for him, as if there was no one else in the world.

And I revelled in it.

His big hand slid down my side, slipping behind me to squeeze my ass.

"Enid love, touch me."

A needy moan slipped from between my lips as I fisted his shirt, tugging it up his body to slide my hands across his bare skin.

Not even Colin Firth emerging from a lake can compare to this.

"Fuck," Henry panted as his hands dipped, gripping my ass and boosting me up. "Fuck."

I followed his unspoken demands, boosting myself up and wrapping my legs around his hips, my core pressed against his crotch.

He pressed me back into the wall, his cock grinding against my sensitive flesh through a pair of jeans and the flimsy material of my underwear.

"Henry, I need—"

He shifted, turning to walk the few steps across the room to the island. With a sweep of one hand, he sent groceries and ingredients toppling to the floor, mindless of the mess he'd created.

"Need to be in you."

He lay me on the cool counter, spreading me wide as he tore my lingerie from my body.

"Your turn," I demanded, ripping his shirt over his head.

As he fumbled with his belt and zip with one hand, he ran fingers between my thighs with his other, his blunt digits finding my wet, aching core.

"Fuck," he broke off our kiss, his fingers gliding deliciously through the wet heat of my naked pussy. "How did we wait so long?"

"Less talk," I panted. "More kissing."

"Happy to oblige."

He caught my mouth once more, our tongues dancing together as he circled my clit, his fingers moving faster and faster, pressing me in a way guaranteed to drive me crazy.

Please.

His fingers disappeared, and I whimpered, arching my hips up, desperate for more. Between us, his hand fumbled at his crotch.

"It's okay, Enid love. Just let me get this fly undone—" His cock pressed to me, deliciously hard, hot and thick. "You ready?"

"'Condom?" I asked, barely able to believe I could think of protection.

"Fuck!"

He ripped himself away from me, stumbling over his jeans as he hurried from the room, leaving me spread across his counter.

I caught sight of myself in the decorative mirror in the dining area, my body laying across the counter like a naked rotisserie chicken.

Well, this isn't at all sexy.

I grew self-conscious, beginning to shift and sit up when he returned, rolling on a condom.

"Fuck," he halted, his hand fisting his cock. "Fuck, you're beautiful. I cannot think when I see you, Enid. You take my breath away."

Oh.

My heart gave up any resistance, gleefully taking the leap of faith.

I love him.

Henry came to me, his cock pressing against my core as he tasted my nipples, sucking them and licking, teasing until I was one aching, moaning body of need.

"Henry!"

He thrust forward, burying himself to the hilt. We both cried out, the friction and heat overwhelming. He fucked into me, and my control broke. I no longer thought of my body or the mess on the floor. My only thought was of Henry. He surrounded me, consumed me with his smell, his feel, and his cock as it drove me higher, chasing my release.

"You like this, Enid love? You like knowing I couldn't wait to make love to you?" Henry asked, holding my hips in place as he thrust into me, my tits bouncing.

"You like knowing I'll be thinking about fucking you every time I walk into this room? You like knowing I'm going to taste every part of you? That I'll lick the sweet cream from between your thighs?"

I nodded, words impossible to form as heat wrapped around me, desire spiking. I dragged fingernails up his back, clawing for more as my orgasm built.

"More?"

I nodded, then gasped when Henry

dropped one hand, his fingers finding my clit. "Henry!"

He fisted my hair, pulling me to him, merging our mouths together as I came. Our tongues tangled, my body milking his cock as he came.

Henry collapsed on top of me, his upper body trapping me against the countertop as we both attempted to slow our breathing.

"You okay?" he asked, pressing a kiss to my shoulder.

"Mm," I hummed. "I can't feel my legs."

He chuckled. "Would you like to go again?"

I blinked. "What?"

"Dinner first," he said, lazily sliding a thumb across my erect nipple. "Then round two."

"I can live with that."

CHAPTER 14

Enid

I woke in Henry's bed, my body deliciously achy.

With a small grin, I stretched, relishing the feel of loose limbs and well-used muscles.

In addition to the counter, we'd christened his couch, his entry table, his shower, and then his bed before I'd finally pleaded for sleep.

He'd woken me with his mouth a few hours ago, then told me to go back to sleep. Considering my office hours didn't start for a little while longer, I had no problem drifting back to sleep.

My cell beeped, alerting me to a notification.

I grinned, expecting to see Henry's name.

LINDA

> Enid, could you come by the office around eleven? I have something I wish to discuss with you.

I sat up, the blankets falling around me as I hit reply.

ENID

> Of course! I'll be there ASAP!

I showered, throwing on the spare clothing I'd brought with me last night, grateful that Kei had insisted I take spares with me.

My phone buzzed as I walked across the campus, headed for the Dean's office.

KEIKO

> I assume your unused bed means you got thoroughly used last night.

I grinned, typing out a quick reply.

ENID

> Oh yes. Keiko… I think he's the one.

KEIKO

!!!!!!! YASSS QUEEN!!! Now,
what are we talking size-wise?
Is he a grower or a show-er? Are
we happy with size or skill? Is
there thickness involved?
Remember, enthusiasm makes
up for a lot.

I laughed, my heart light even as anxiety churned in my belly.

I paused at the Dean's office doors, taking a fortifying breath.

But what if you don't get it?

I closed my eyes, imagining my life.

Henry's face rose in my mind, his laughing grin easy to recall.

I'd still have him.

"I want it," I whispered to myself, admitting my deepest desires. "I want the job. But I want Henry and the life we could have even more. The job won't keep me warm at night. It's not going to hold me when things are tough or make me laugh. My career can weather this. If this isn't the position for me, then so be it. I'll live. I'll love. I'll move on."

I tested how that felt, knowing I needed to be honest with myself.

There's no room for regret or resentment in this relationship.

Surprisingly, I felt nothing but anxious hope.

"Whatever will be, will be."

I shoved open the door, finding the Dean's secretary at her desk.

"Enid, hello! She's expecting you, go on in."

I knocked gently, waiting on her to call me in.

"Enid, hello, please sit."

I took one of the chairs across from her, settling in, my heart a loud beat in my ears.

Linda knit her fingers together, pressing them to her chin as she considered me.

"Enid, I'm going to cut to the chase, we offered Henry Phillip's position and he's accepted. He's agreed to keep it quiet until the paperwork is settled but I expect that we'll be able to announce at the faculty meeting next week."

My breath punched out of my lungs, tears burning the back of my eyes as I tried to keep my composure.

That explains his mood last night.

God, this felt like the most bittersweet moment I'd ever experienced. The man I loved had swooped in to take the job I'd wanted for more than a decade. But at the same time, Henry's acceptance of the position meant that he was staying. That he wanted to stay. That we could have a future together.

What a complex world we live in.

"I wanted to thank you for your application but at the end of the day, I think Henry is a better fit for this position."

I nodded, smoothing out the skirt of my dress before rising. "I understand. Thank you for letting me know."

"Enid, sit down. We're not done."

I frowned, resuming my seat.

"While Henry is a better fit for this position, I've been working on getting more money for the school." She slid a sheet of paper across my desk. "Do you remember when you pitched to me the Master's program last year?"

I nodded. "You said there was no funding available."

"Well, that's changed. With Henry signing on, we have an opportunity to capitalise on his star and gain additional support for the new courses." She leaned across the desk. "I want you to lead their development."

I stared at Linda unable to comprehend the change in my fortune.

"You want me to...."

"To become my newest head of department." She tapped the paper. "This is your contract. It's a tenured position, Enid. If you're interested."

Joy, pure and unadulterated, surged through my body. This was everything—no, it was *more* than everything—I'd ever dreamed of.

"Yes! A hundred million times, yes, yes, yes!"

Linda laughed, sitting back in her chair. "Fantastic. I have to admit, when you applied for Phillip's job, I was very concerned that you wouldn't be interested in this one. But I think it's a much better fit for you."

"Absolutely. Thank you, Linda. I promise I won't let you down."

"I'd never doubt it."

CHAPTER 15

Enid

I floated on air to the research lab, desperate to find Henry and share my good news.

I found him bent over one of the storage boxes, pouring over diaries and letters.

"Hello, Enid love," he greeted, coming to kiss me with a passion that I adored.

I ducked my head a little, flushing as I remembered the last time I'd seen him. He'd been licking my clit with a determination that had to be rewarded.

"Missed you," he said, pulling me in for a hug. "You look radiant today."

A girl could get used to this.

I knew I wasn't what he saw. I wasn't the

kind of stunning beauty that stopped people in their tracks. But I didn't need to be—all I needed was for Henry to see me as such. And I'd never been so grateful that he did.

"What has you glowing today, hmm?"

I grinned, knowing I was about to simultaneously delight him, and deflate his ego.

"As much as I wish it was just you," I said, giving him a squeeze. "It's actually a meeting I just had with the Dean." I leaned into him. "Henry, I have to admit something."

"Okay."

"I wanted Phillip's job. Badly. I applied and I was devastated this morning to learn that you'd been offered it instead of me."

He froze his face a picture of horror. "Fuck! Enid! Fuck. I'm so sorry. I didn't realize—of course it should be you." He stepped away from me, turning to leave. "I'll go right now to Linda and explain—"

I caught his arm, tugging him back to me, happiness making me giddy.

This wonderful man is mine. All mine.

"But that's just it, if you quit then you'll have to leave. Henry." I reached up, cupping his cheek, our gazes locked. "I don't want that to happen. Ever."

"I could write instead," he said, his expression fierce. "And I could guest lecture."

"But let's be honest, your heart is in the research." I gestured at the storage boxes around us. "I wouldn't be much of a wife if I didn't support your dream."

His body stilled. "Wife?"

Time to lay it on the line.

"One day, if you'll have me."

"Any day. Today. Yes! Enid love." Henry's voice broke, his arms clamping around me as he practically strangled me. "Yes!"

I laughed, pressing kisses to his cheeks as he swung me around.

"But what about your dream?" he asked, returning me to the floor.

"Oh, that." I burst out laughing, unable to hide my delight. "I'm tenured! I'm the newest head of the department. Everything I've ever wanted has happened today, Henry. I'm just so happy I could burst!"

He caught my lips, tasting the joy. "Proud of you, Enid love."

Our kisses quickly escalated to groping, then hands slipping under clothing to touch heated skin. Before I knew it, Henry had laid me out on his long desk, shoving boxes out of the way as he fisted my skirts, revealing my underwear.

"Shit. Condom."

"I'm clear and on the pill," I panted, desperate for him.

"I'm clear," he admitted, fumbling with his fly. "Is this okay?"

"More than."

A finger pulled my underwear to one side, his cock pressing hard and hot against me.

"Fucking love you," Henry whispered against my ear. His hot breath sent shivers down my spine as he began to ease his length inside me, stretching my inner muscles. "You're the other half of my soul, Enid love."

"I love you," I whispered, a tear slipping free. "More than anything."

We made love on his research table, the desk rocking back and forth with his thrusts, our bodies heated, mouths desperate as we came in a noisy, glorious mess.

A storage box fell from the table, the contents spilling across the floor.

"Damn," I whispered, closing my eyes. "We should pick that up."

"Mm, in a minute. I just want to hold you first."

I allowed him to do just that, our arms wrapped tight around each other, our bodies pressed together, sharing space and giving comfort.

"Alright," I said finally, laughing as I shoved

him away. "We need to clean this up then I need to get to class."

On hands and knees, we chased papers down, gently smoothing them out and placing them in the box.

I picked up a handwritten letter, a name catching my eye as I went to return it.

Mary Allen.

I froze, my body seizing as I read the letter.

My Dearest Sarah,

I dare say you would be much disappointed in the accommodation I secured upon my arrival. Dreadfully dirty and filled with pests the kind of which I'd not had experience with.

I'd hoped to find Astipia filled with possibility. Alas, a woman isn't of much value here, my Sarah. And a woman who thinks? It

seems the men aren't much better
than those back home.
I've made peace with this and have
instead come up with a rather daring
plan. I'll adopt the persona of
Cedric Cagle, a successful author,
and man about town. I'll send for
you shortly, and we'll marry, no one
the wiser.
If I'd thought we could live
without judgement, if I'd thought I
could publish my writings under my
own name, then I would. But
etiquette demands that we remain
civil and adopt a woman's place. No
matter how much that noose chaffs
our neck.
If becoming Cedric is what is
required for us to love freely, I do
so willingly and willfully.
I love you, my Sarah.
Until we are reunited again.

Yours,
Mary Allen.

My hand shook as I looked up, finding Henry flicking through a diary.

"Henry." My voice sounded strange, even to my own ears.

"What? What's wrong? Did you hurt yourself?"

I shook my head, words eluding me as I handed him the letter. "Read."

He took it, scanning the contents, his eyes widening as he came to the end.

"This is...."

"I know."

"Enid, do you have any idea what this means?"

I nodded tears in my eyes. "It's proof. You were right. Cedric is Mary."

"And she wanted to be known for her works."

"And Sarah. They married. All of it, you were right."

Henry burst out laughing, pulling me in to kiss me.

"I love you."

"And I love you, Henry." I pointed to the letter. "Now go write the paper that will give Ms. Mary the recognition she deserves."

EPILOGUE

Henry

Two Years Later

"And now the groom will read a passage from Mary Allen's poem, *Bride O' Mine*."

I squeezed Enid's hands, grinning at my beautiful bride.

"Bride of my heart. Bride of my life. Wife you will be, and I your groom. Our marriage intertwined; our love forever carved in stone. You are my heart, my dearest one. You own my soul, my body, my mind. With rings we wed, this day we share, this love of ours, this life we

lead, Bride 'o mine, together it is known as joy."

A single tear ran down Enid's cheek, her smile radiant.

"You may now kiss the bride."

I leaned in, catching Enid's mouth, tasting her as around us family and friends burst into raucous applause.

Reluctantly I pulled back, pressing my forehead to hers.

"Hello, wife." The title had never tasted so sweet.

"Hello, husband."

"Are you ready for this adventure?" I asked.

"I've never been more ready for anything in my life."

Enid froze, her body tensing.

"Enid?"

She pulled away from me, stepping back to lift her skirts. Wet soaked the wood floor of the library, her body shaking as she began to laugh, her pregnant belly bobbing.

"It seems," she said, laughter in her voice. "That our son also cannot wait."

Panic overrode all my emotions.

"You're in labour!" I turned to our guests. "She's in labour!"

There was a flurry of skirts and movement as people attempted to help.

A half-hour later, safely bundled in the back of an ambulance, Enid gripped my hand, smiling at me.

"Shall we call him Cedric?"

"God no, the bullying he'll get," I scoffed, shaking my head.

"How about Rick then?"

I considered that option. "What about Allen?"

"Oh, I like that."

And so, hours later, the most beautiful woman in the world delivered our baby and made me the happiest man in the world.

Thank you so much for reading Henry and Enid's story!

You can continue the entire series by checking them out on my website at www. EvieMitchell.com

If you enter the code **EBOOK10** *you can get 10% off your purchase from my website.*

Be sure to also sign up for my newsletter or check out my website for more book news.

ABOUT THE AUTHOR

Hey, I'm Evie Mitchell.
I'm a thirty-something romance author (she/her/hers) living with disability. I believe in inclusion, accessibility, and fierce romance. My loves include steamy romance novels, my sexy husband, our THREE sausage dogs (THE FUR!!!), and my ever-growing collection of book-related mugs.

As a woman with a diverse work history, including in areas such as hospitality, retail, emergency response, event management, human rights, disability access, and security— my books are filled with true stories (bridezillas), worst-case scenarios (malfunctioning zippers), and my favorite tropes (one-bed).

I'm a strong proponent of #OwnVoices, and specialize in fiercely inclusive happily ever afters.

EvieMitchell.com
Socials: @EvieMitchellAuthor

As You Wish
You Sleigh Me
Meat Load
Resolution Revolution

Dogg Pack

Puppy Love
The Frock Up
Pier Pressure
Trick or Trent
New Year's Faye

Reigning Hearts

The Marriage Claim
Silent Knight

Men of Trinity Bay

Kink in the Road

Nameless Souls MC

Runner
Wrath
Ghost
Shield

Elliot Security

Rough Edge

Bleeding Edge